STEPHEN HAWKING

MARY-LANE KAMBERG

ROSEN
PUBLISHING®

New York

For Ann Nelson

Published in 2015 by The Rosen Publishing Group, Inc.

29 East 21st Street, New York, NY 10010
Copyright © 2015 by The Rosen Publishing Group, Inc.

First Edition

Library of Congress Cataloging-in-Publication Data

Kamberg, Mary-Lane, 1948– author.
Stephen Hawking/Mary-Lane Kamberg.—First edition.
        pages cm.—(Great science writers)
Includes bibliographical references and index.
ISBN 978-1-4777-7683-4 (library bound)
1. Hawking, Stephen, 1942-—Juvenile literature.
2. Physicists—Great Britain—Biography—Juvenile literature.
3. Scientists—Great Britain—Biography—Juvenile literature.
4. Black holes (Astronomy)—Juvenile literature. I. Title.
QC16.H33K36 2015
539.092—dc23
                                            2013043306

Manufactured in China

CONTENTS

INTRODUCTION

H is teachers thought him a slacker, while his friends called him "Einstein." Some know him as that scientist who has a severe physical disability. Others call him "the most brilliant cosmologist of our age" and a "supreme communicator to lay readers of extremely difficult physical concepts." Stephen William Hawking is best known, however, as the theoretical physicist who brought science to everyone. Known for his razor-sharp wit, Hawking has lectured to sold-out audiences around the world.

Hawking's accomplishments are all the more notable because of the obstacles he has had to overcome. Shortly after entering Cambridge University, Hawking was diagnosed with

4

Stephen William Hawking, one of the world's great science writers, has found a way to continue conducting research and writing in spite of disabilities caused by amyotrophic lateral sclerosis (ALS).

amyotrophic lateral sclerosis (ALS), a disabling disease that kills nerve cells in the brain and spinal cord, and is known as motor neuron disease in Britain. At the age of twenty-one, he had a life expectancy of only two years.

Hawking decided to make the most of the time he believed he had left. He earned a doctorate, married twice, and had three children. His pioneering work on black holes and the beginning of space and time have revolutionized the way scientists and nonscientists alike view the universe.

Among the more than two hundred academic papers and books he has published during his lifetime—he defied the doctors' dire predictions of life expectancy, celebrating his seventy-first birthday in the summer of 2013—are several books written for the mass market, wherein Hawking explains the universe to the general public. Hawking published his first and best-known popular work, *A Brief History of Time*, in 1988. According to Kristine Larsen in *Stephen Hawking: A Biography*, the book, which was published in three dozen languages, has sold more than two hundred million copies.

Since then, Hawking has written a dozen more books, including three for children. In short, he is not only one of the greatest scientific minds of all time but one of the greatest science writers as well.

CHAPTER ONE

AN UNLIKELY SCIENCE SUPERSTAR

A time traveler going back to England in the mid-1950s might ask the teachers at St. Albans High School for Boys to name which of their students would become one of the world's greatest science writers. Chances are none would guess Stephen Hawking. Despite exhibiting boundless curiosity as a schoolboy, Hawking was a mediocre student. Eventually, however, he would live

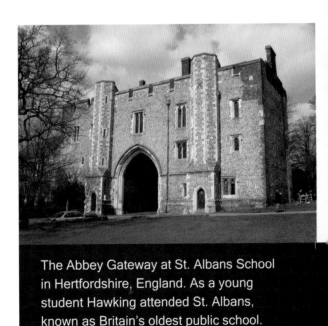

The Abbey Gateway at St. Albans School in Hertfordshire, England. As a young student Hawking attended St. Albans, known as Britain's oldest public school.

up to the nickname bestowed upon him by some of his friends—Einstein.

THE BIRTH OF A STAR

Stephen's parents, Isobel and Frank, met at a medical research institute in Hampstead, England, where she was working as a secretary and he was a researcher of tropical diseases. Isobel, whose father was a family doctor in Glasgow, Scotland, had studied philosophy, politics, and economics at Oxford University, graduating at a time when few women pursued higher education. Frank's farming family hailed from Yorkshire in northern England. Once prosperous, they bought too much land and fell on hard times around the turn of the century. Still, they managed to save enough to send their son to Oxford.

The two married, and Isobel became pregnant in the spring of 1941. During her pregnancy, German pilots regularly bombed London, England, where she and her husband lived. Wanting her first child born in safety, Isobel sought out a new place to call home. According to rumor, Germany and Britain had agreed not to bomb certain cities in each other's countries. They spared the university towns of Oxford and Cambridge in England and Heidelberg and Gottingen in Germany. Isobel temporarily relocated to Oxford, and it was there that Stephen was born.

A COSMIC CONNECTION

Stephen William Hawking's birth on January 8, 1942, created speculation about metaphysical coincidence, as the date marked the three-hundredth anniversary of Galileo Galilei's death. Many consider the seventeenth-century Italian physicist, mathematician, astronomer, and philosopher to be the world's first true scientist. He was best known for proposing a new way to look at the universe; nearly four centuries later, so was Hawking. As an adult, Hawking failed to acknowledge his birth date's significance. On his official Web site, he said, "I estimate that about two hundred thousand other babies were also born that day. I don't know whether any of them were later interested in astronomy."

Fans of the eerie also point to the fact that as a child, Hawking claimed to own a house other than the family home in Oxford, claiming it was located in a

Portrait of Galileo Galilei. Galileo and Hawking each introduced new ways of understanding the universe, four hundred years apart.

place called Drane. He begged his parents to let him board a bus to go look for the stately home he had seen in a dream. Isobel, who often took the children to London's museums and art galleries, assumed her

The dining room at Kenwood House. When Hawking's mother took him to see the art displayed at the house in London, he told her that it was his "other" house that he had seen in a dream.

son's imagination was on the loose. However, one day she took her children to London's Kenwood House, a restored, early eighteenth-century building full of paintings by the old masters. Young Stephen identified Kenwood House as the stately home he had envisioned while he slept.

ALL IN THE FAMILY

Hawking's early years were spent in the London suburb of Highgate, where his sister Mary was born in 1943. During the war, his father became head of the Division of Parasitology at the National Institute of Medical Research in Mill Hill, a northern London suburb.

Hawking began his education at age four at Byron House School. The school's philosophy was to let students learn at their own speed—a method that didn't work for the young boy. Many years later, he wrote on his Web site, "I remember complaining to my parents that [the teachers] weren't teaching me anything."

Hawking's second sister, Philippa, arrived in 1947, when he was five. Three years later, the family moved to a three-story Victorian house in the city of St.

GALILEO GALILEI

Stephen Hawking was born on the three-hundredth anniversary of the death of Italian scientist Galileo Galilei. However, the date is only one of many things the two scientists have in common. Both men's fathers wanted their sons to study medicine. Both were drawn to the study of mathematics and were bored with their university studies. After completing their respective educations, they taught in universities. They each offered new views of the universe and proposed controversial theories. Finally, both wrote scientific books that were accessible to ordinary citizens.

Galileo's book *The Starry Messenger*, published in 1610, detailed what he had discovered while gazing at the night sky through his new device, the telescope. The book received wide acclaim. A later work, *Dialogue Concerning the Two Chief World Systems, Ptolemaic and Copernican*, was another popular read—at least until it was banned by the Roman Catholic Church during the seventeenth-century Inquisition.

In 1633, Galileo was accused of heresy and summoned to Rome, where church elders demanded that he renounce the Copernican theory of the universe. In a public confession, Galileo said that he had overstated his case. He lived out the remainder of his life under what could be called house arrest.

Albans, 20 miles (32 kilometers) north of London. Hawking enjoyed exploring the new house. He could jump from his bedroom window to the roof of a bicycle shed. He eventually discovered eleven ways to enter and leave the house without using the front door. (His sister Mary later reported she had found only ten of them.)

Their new neighbors must have thought the family a bit strange. The Hawkings drove a used taxi, made their own fireworks, and kept bees for honey. Their old house had no central heat and was constantly in need of repairs. Broken windows, peeling wallpaper, and worn carpet were neither fixed nor replaced. Instead the parents explored their own interests, filling the house with books, which they and the children often silently read during dinner.

At times it was difficult to understand Hawking— not because his ideas were unreasonably complex, but because he had difficulty speaking. He had a bit of a lisp, and his rapid-fire delivery was hard to follow. In fact, many people had trouble comprehending the whole Hawking family. Stephen's father stammered, and all the members spoke quickly. Friends nicknamed the family's style of speech "Hawkingese."

Frank Hawking introduced his children to science, including astronomy. The whole family enjoyed lying

An expansive view of the Milky Way, as seen from the Rocky Desert in Nevada. As a child, Hawking loved to look at the night sky through his father's telescope.

on the lawn and looking at the night sky through a telescope. The young boy was especially awed by a view of the Milky Way Galaxy. Isobel Hawking introduced the family to social issues. She had joined the Communist Party during the war, and afterward she participated in protests and labor strikes. She also worked to ensure that the type of nuclear weapons that ended World War II in Japan would never again be used anywhere.

THE LEARNING CURVE

Soon after the Hawkings moved to St. Albans, Stephen entered the St. Albans High School for Girls. The school admitted both boys and girls younger than ten. Hawking's future wife Jane Wilde attended the same school. She later said she had seen Stephen there but never met him.

Frank Hawking spent his winters in Africa researching mosquito-borne diseases. The first winter after the family had moved to the new house, Isobel took the children to the Spanish island of Majorca for a four-month visit with her longtime friend Beryl Graves and her husband, the poet Robert Graves. While there, Stephen Hawking and the Graveses' son shared a tutor, who assigned daily Bible readings and had them write reports about what they had read. The two boys made it through Genesis and part of Exodus before the Hawkings left for home.

When the family returned to St. Albans, young Hawking spent a year at a private school called Radlett. After that, he took a scholarship test at St. Albans and earned a free education at St. Albans High School; by then he was old enough to attend the school for boys. In 1956, his parents adopted another son, Edward.

BOYS' CLUB

Despite exhibiting boundless curiosity, Hawking was a mediocre student. As a schoolboy, he often felt like an outsider. He couldn't read until the age of eight, and his handwriting was impossible to read. He never enjoyed sports, although he liked long bike rides. Fortunately he had a few friends who shared his interests. While most of their schoolmates played sports outside, he and his friends stayed in and invented complicated board games that took hours or days to play. The board for their war game based on World War II had four thousand squares. One game, called Dynasty, seemingly went on forever, largely because the rules, written primarily by Hawking, failed to provide any way to win or even to end the game. According to Melissa McDaniel in

Stephen Hawking: Revolutionary Physicist, a friend from that time said, "Stephen loved the fact that he had created the world and then created the laws that governed it."

The boys dealt with complex ideas and mathematical formulas in Hawking's bedroom, which housed several advanced math and science textbooks, as well as test tubes and other equipment needed for experiments. Hawking enjoyed conversation about many topics. He and his friends often talked about chemistry, politics, and religion. In fact, the entire Hawking family frequently debated religious topics, particularly for and against the existence of God.

Although Hawking was a bit clumsy and never had much skill with his hands, that didn't stop him from building model boats and airplanes in a friend's father's workshop. Rather than being concerned about building the models to exact specifications, Hawking put his efforts into making them work. Electronics also drew his interest. He once tried to turn a television into an amplifier and got a 500-volt shock for his trouble. Undeterred, he built his own record player with inexpensive parts, using it to enjoy a pricey recording of a Brahms violin concerto he had purchased.

In 1958, Hawking and his friends got help from their sophomore math teacher to build a simple computer from used telephone switchboards. (It would be at least twenty years before computers revolutionized calculation and communication.) It took them a month to complete and perfect the machine, which its inventors called the Logical Uniselector Computing Engine, LUCE for short. The school newspaper, the *Albanian*, reported on their accomplishment: "The machine answers some useless, though quite complex, logical problems." Later, the boys left LUCE behind and built another, better computer that could add, subtract, multiply, and divide.

CHAPTER TWO

REACHING FOR THE STARS

s Stephen entered his last two years at St. Albans, he began to think about his future. He had always thought he would pursue a career in science. So did his father. However, the two disagreed on which branch of science Stephen should study. His father wanted him to attend Oxford and become a doctor, but Stephen had no interest in biology. His math teacher had inspired him, and so he wanted to study mathematics. Frank Hawking thought the only future for a mathematician was in teaching, so he encouraged his son to take chemistry instead in order to keep his options open.

Frank Hawking had another academic goal for his eldest child; he wanted Stephen to attend either the University of Oxford or the University of Cambridge. Since Stephen's parents both had graduated from

Oxford, Frank Hawking thought his son would have a better chance of being accepted there. Unfortunately for Stephen, Oxford had no mathematics program.

A panoramic view of Oxford University. Although Oxford is one of the world's best universities, Hawking complained that his studies were boring and too easy.

Instead, he applied for a scholarship in natural science, which included astronomy and physics. After a year preparing for the Oxford entrance exam, he got high scores on the physics portion of the test. He won the scholarship and entered the university at the age of seventeen, all set to study physics and the universe.

BORED BUT EXCELLING

Records show that instructors were teaching at Oxford as early as 1096. As such, the school is the world's oldest English-speaking university. Despite its reputation, it was not a good place for Stephen to learn about the cosmos. For one thing, the curriculum bored him, and he found his classes "ridiculously easy." Also, Hawking was younger than most of his fellow students. Many of them had completed military service before entering the university. To make matters worse, he was one of only four physics students in his class. He spent his first year feeling lonely and set apart from the university culture.

Hawking never took notes in class, and he never even bought most of the required textbooks. "One could get through without going to any lectures, just by going to one or two tutorials a week," he said in Kristine Larsen's biography *Stephen Hawking*. "You didn't need to remember many facts, just a few equations."

His three physics classmates disagreed. It took them nearly a week to complete one of thirteen homework problems, while Hawking had worked ten in a single morning, on the same day they were due.

ROWING ON THE RIVER

Things got better the next year. Classwork remained easy; Hawking estimates he spent only about an hour a day studying. The difference came about in his social life. Although Hawking was a small, decidedly nonathletic student, he attended the recruiting party for the university's crew club.

One member of the rowing team remembered meeting Hawking there. In *Stephen Hawking: Breaking the Boundaries of Time and Space*, teammate David Firth was quoted as saying, "Eight of the rugby team, including me, stood uneasily on board the beautiful old college barge, waiting to try our hands at rowing for the first time ... It soon dawned on me that we were not alone. A much smaller figure stood alongside our group, distinguished by a blazer instead of a rugby shirt, huge dark horn-rimmed spectacles, and an immaculate straw [hat]."

Rowing teams consisted of eight rowers and a coxswain, or the one in charge of the boat. As the coxswain, Hawking sat in the boat's bow and steered, controlling the team's stroke rate by shouting

Members of the 2005 Oxford rowing team being coached on the Thames River. Hawking won a place as the team's coxswain, shouting commands to control the oarsmen's stroke rate.

commands and cheers of support. He didn't have to row, so he needed no physical strength, and his light weight was an advantage.

The burly rugby players were strong but lacked the endurance needed to sustain their energy for the length of a race. Still, they worked hard, as did Hawking. One of his crew later recalled in Stephanie McPherson's *Stephen Hawking*, "Stephen refused to give up on any of us, and somehow convinced us by the day of our first race that we were not quite so hopeless after all."

Crew was a popular sport at the university, and it became a stepping-stone to Hawking's improved social life. Other students noticed him and appreciated his sense of humor and adventure. He started to share his love of music and science fiction. In short, he began to fit in.

The team became more important to him than classwork. Hawking devoted himself to the sport. The team practiced on the Thames River six afternoons a week in all weather conditions, even when a thin sheet of ice covered the water. Afternoons were also the times set for work in the university lab, so Hawking wound up spending less time doing experiments. He cut corners when it came to collecting data and used his "creativity" to complete lab reports.

TIME TO BUCKLE DOWN

During Hawking's third year at Oxford, he fell down a flight of stairs and landed on his head. He temporarily lost both his short-term and long-term memory. He soon recovered, though, and gave little thought to the incident.

Instead he again considered his future. He looked forward to study toward a Ph.D. in cosmology, but Oxford did not offer what he was looking for. However, England's other major university, Cambridge, did. Sir Frederick Hoyle, Britain's most distinguished astronomer, taught there, and Hawking wanted to study with him.

Admission to Cambridge would require a first-class degree from Oxford. A final exam determined which of four classes of degree the university would award. In his last semester, however, Hawking realized that he was nowhere near ready for the test. He knew that it was time to buckle down and study.

Renowned astronomer Sir Frederick Hoyle, in the 1950s. Hawking sought to study under Hoyle at Cambridge.

Hawking could not learn everything he needed to in the few months he had left, so he devised a strategy. He concentrated his efforts on theoretical physics because that way he wasn't held to knowing a bunch of facts. In a pinch, he could use his imagination. He would be graded only on questions he answered, and there was no penalty for skipping a question. So instead of guessing, he planned to skip questions he couldn't answer.

When the test results were posted, Hawking's score landed him in the middle between achieving a first-class and a second-class degree. Hawking met with Oxford faculty, who would determine which degree he received. One professor asked what Hawking would do after he graduated. Hawking replied that he wanted to conduct research. Then, knowing that his reputation as a poor, distracted student had followed him to Oxford, he said that if he got a first-class degree he would go to Cambridge, but if he got a second he would stay at Oxford. The Oxford faculty awarded him a first. Hawking later commented that he never knew if their decision was based on his own wishes or their wish to be rid of him.

He was accepted to Cambridge University for further study in the Department of Applied Mathematics and Theoretical Physics. Upon arrival at the university in 1962, Hawking was again disappointed. Hoyle, the astronomer whom he had hoped to work with, had

Cambridge University professor Dennis Sciama. When Hawking studied under him, Sciama was relatively unknown. However, he later became known as one of the fathers of modern cosmology.

too many graduate students. Instead, Hawking was assigned to lesser-known Dennis Sciama to pursue his studies.

On his Web site, Hawking has stated that the situation was "probably for the best. Hoyle was away a lot, seldom in the department, and I wouldn't have had much of his attention. Sciama, on the other hand, was usually around and ready to talk. I didn't agree with many of his ideas ... but that stimulated me to develop my own picture."

At the time cosmology was yet to become an established field of study. However, Sciama later became known as one of the fathers of modern cosmology. He helped the field gain acceptance as a mainstream branch of physics.

A FALLING STAR

When Hawking went home to St. Albans for Christmas break during his first year at Cambridge, his father immediately noticed a difference in his son's speech. The younger Hawking slurred, and his "Hawkingese" was harder to understand. In addition, he was clumsy and often tripped. His parents insisted that he see the family doctor, who referred him to a specialist for medical tests after the first of the year.

Meanwhile Hawking was ready to party. He went to a New Year's Day gathering at a friend's

WHAT IS ALS?

Amyotrophic lateral sclerosis, or ALS, is a disabling disease that kills nerve cells in the brain and spinal cord. Muscle weakness is an early sign. As the disease progresses, slurred speech, tripping, and clumsiness are classic symptoms.

People with ALS become unable to control voluntary muscle movement throughout the body. Speech and swallowing become increasingly difficult. Involuntary muscle movement, such as the beating of the heart, however, is not affected. Neither is the brain. Most people who get ALS live only three to five years. However, some, like Stephen Hawking, survive for decades.

In the United States, ALS is also called Lou Gehrig's disease. Lou Gehrig was a New York Yankees first baseman and National Baseball Hall of Famer. He retired from baseball when he was diagnosed with the disease in 1939.

home, where he met Jane Wilde. In her book *Music to Move the Stars*, Wilde described Hawking at their first meeting as being "slight of frame." She recalled that he was wearing a black-velvet jacket

Hawking met his future wife Jane Wilde at a New Year's Day party during the graduate student's winter break during his first year at Cambridge.

and red-velvet bow tie, and that his hair fell across his face, over his glasses.

Hawking entertained her with the story of convincing Oxford examiners to give him a first-class degree. Although she enjoyed Hawking's sense of humor and curiosity, Wilde suspected there was a touch of shyness hiding behind his outgoing personality. He also told her he was studying cosmology, but she had no idea what that was. A few days later, Hawking invited her to his twenty-first birthday party. A rather shy woman herself, Wilde spent most of the party sitting in a corner.

Hawking experienced more physical problems during the party. Guests noticed he had trouble pouring beverages for his friends. Soon after he entered St. Bartholomew's Hospital. After two weeks of medical tests, the diagnosis was unclear. Doctors ruled out multiple sclerosis, an autoimmune disease that kills nerve cells. They told him to return to Cambridge and continue his research.

Still, Hawking could tell something was wrong. In *Stephen Hawking: An Unfettered Mind*, he was quoted as saying, "I gathered that they expected [my condition] to continue to get worse, and there was nothing they could do, except give me vitamins. I could see that they didn't expect them to have much effect. I didn't feel like asking for more details because they were obviously bad."

Somehow, the most serious news was kept from Hawking's mother. During the holiday break she and her son went ice-skating. He fell and couldn't get up. Isobel Hawking helped him stand and got him to a nearby café. She asked him to level with her about his condition, then called the doctor herself for more details. The diagnosis was an incurable condition called motor neuron disease in the United Kingdom. In the United States it's known as amyotrophic lateral sclerosis (ALS), or Lou Gehrig's disease.

Hawking's prognosis was devastating. At the time, most people with the disease lived only two years after diagnosis. Hawking wrote, "The realization that I had an incurable disease that was likely to kill me in a few years, was a bit of a shock. How could something like that happen to me?"

The news caused him to experience a serious bout of depression. However, while he was in the hospital, the boy in the next bed died of leukemia. "Clearly," he wrote, "there were people who were worse off than I. Whenever I feel inclined to be sorry for myself, I remember that boy."

THE BIG BANG

Before Hawking knew his diagnosis, life had bored him. He had thought nothing was worth making an effort for. On his Web site he had noted that his illness changed all that. "When you are faced with the possibility of an early death," he wrote, "it makes you realize that life is worth living, and that there are lots of things you want to do."

One of the things Hawking wanted to do was to date Jane Wilde. On their first date he took her out to dinner at a nice Italian restaurant and the theater. They dated off and on after that, often going to the opera.

While Hawking continued his research at Cambridge, his father contacted experts in diseases related to ALS. Frank Hawking found little hope of treatment or cure. He contacted Dennis Sciama, Hawking's adviser, and asked him to help Stephen finish his doctoral thesis early. The adviser refused.

CURIOUS ABOUT THE COSMOS

Hawking had a choice of two areas for his doctoral research, elementary particle physics or cosmology. More academic activity was happening in elementary particle physics. The world's best scientists were working in the field and frequently reported new ideas and discoveries. Research in cosmology was far less active—so that's what Hawking chose.

He realized, however, that he needed some additional education. Despite his interest in mathematics in high school, he had not learned anything new in the field at Oxford. He had already known all the math he needed there. At Cambridge, he had to play catch-up. He also needed to know more about Einstein's theory of relativity. He traveled to London every week to attend lectures on the subject at Kings College. While in London, he often took the opportunity to see Wilde.

Kings College at Cambridge University, where Hawking attended weekly lectures that furthered his education.

A STEADY STATE?

In the early 1960s, the big controversy in cosmology was whether the universe always was, and would always be, or if it had had a definitive starting point. Two schools of thought had emerged. One sought to prove that the universe had a beginning. Sir Frederick Hoyle, who scoffed at the idea, called it "the Big Bang." The other viewpoint, which was proposed by Hoyle and others, was the steady state theory, which maintained that the universe had no beginning and would have no end. This theory further proposed that the average density of the universe is and always has been constant because new matter replaces matter that disappears as the universe expands. Proponents thought that if the universe began at some point in the past (as put forth by Big Bang theorists), science would have to account for the idea that the hand of God was involved in creation. That idea didn't lend itself to experiments using the scientific method.

When Hawking began his work, scientists were already challenging the steady state theory. The Radio Astronomy Group at Cavendish Laboratory in Cambridge had discovered faint microwave radiation that likely came from outside the galaxy. Their data showed that the density of the universe had been higher—not constant—in the distant past, thus contradicting the steady state theory. Although the data failed to prove the Big Bang, it showed that the universe formerly had a phase of contraction and that it had quickly expanded.

Sciama sided with Hoyle in supporting the steady state theorists. During Hawking's spring term in 1964, Hoyle was working on ways to modify the theory of general relativity to account for the Radio Astronomy Group's observations. A fellow graduate student named Jayant Narlikar was working with Hoyle on the calculations. Narlikar showed the

Astrophysicist Jayant V. Narlikar, teaching in 1987. In 1964, Hawking discredited calculations Narlikar and Professor Hoyle had made regarding the theory of general relativity.

equations to Hawking, who studied them and did some math of his own.

That June, Hawking attended a meeting of the Royal Society, a respected academy of the world's best scientists, many of whom had won Nobel Prizes. Hoyle was there to present his and Narlikar's as-yet-unpublished work. At the end of the presentation, Hoyle asked for questions. Hawking stood, balancing on his cane. He told Hoyle his numbers were wrong. When Hoyle asked how Hawking knew that, Hawking said he had worked the problems himself. As it turned out, Hawking was right.

WORKING FOR THE FUTURE

In October 1964, Hawking proposed to Wilde. The engagement meant he had something to live for. It also meant he needed to get a job in order to support his soon-to-be wife. He hoped for a paid research position, but first he had to finish his thesis. That meant he would have to study hard.

To Hawking's surprise, he enjoyed the hard work. In fact, it didn't seem like work at all. He wrote up his corrections to Hoyle and Narlikar's work and submitted them to the Royal Society for publication. The society published Hawking's first scientific paper, "On the Hoyle-Narlikar Theory of Gravitation," in 1965.

Hawking decided to focus his research on the properties of an expanding universe. He still had no specific topic for his dissertation, but an idea soon presented itself. Roger Penrose, a mathematician from Birkbeck College in London, had also studied under Sciama at Cambridge. During that time Penrose developed an interest in physics and cosmology. Hawking had heard about him from a fellow graduate student. Hawking's friend had attended a seminar at Kings College, where Penrose spoke. The friend told Hawking that Penrose had applied mathematics to black holes, which are places in space where gravity is so strong that light cannot escape. They form when stars run out of fuel. Their own gravity contracts the remaining matter into a dense body.

Before Penrose's work, physicists knew

Mathematician Roger Penrose, whose work gave Hawking the idea for his graduate thesis, which used mathematics to prove the Big Bang theory.

that Einstein's theory of general relativity allowed for singularities, which were defined as infinitely dense points where space and time failed to exist and the laws of physics no longer applied. However, few thought singularities were likely to exist. Penrose proved that a black hole must contain a singularity.

Hawking thought about Penrose's results and wondered if the mathematician's techniques could apply to the entire universe. Hawking sought to prove that a singularity existed before the universe was formed. Using mathematics to analyze the issue, and including his findings in his thesis, he showed that the universe had indeed begun with a bang—a big one.

INGS

ly for a
nville
e, part of
nt secured,
965. Hawking
s ALS diag-
ted that they
refused to let
ahead with
their lives. Hawking adopted a new attitude, considering each day important.

ACADEMIC WORKS

Stephen Hawking's academic writings published in respected scientific journals enhanced his reputation in the scientific community. In addition to "On the Hoyle-Narlikar Theory of Gravitation" and "Singularities and the Geometry of Space-Time," his more important academic works include:

- "The Singularities of Gravitational Collapse and Cosmology," *Proceedings of the Royal Society A: Mathematical, Physical and Engineering Sciences*, with Roger Penrose, 1970.
- "Gravitational Radiation from Colliding Black Holes," *Physical Review Letters*, 1971.
- "Black Holes in General Relativity," *Communications in Mathematical Physics*, 1972.
- "Black Hole Explosions?" *Nature*, 1974
- "The Development of Irregularities in a Single Bubble Inflationary Universe," *Physics Letters B*, 1982.
- "Wave Function of the Universe," *Physical Review*, with J. Hartle, 1983.
- "Information Loss in Black Holes," *Physical Review*, 2005.

Hawking became a professor at the Institute for Theoretical Astronomy and, deciding that he could best study mathematics by teaching it, he also took a job as a teacher at the Department of Applied Mathematics and Theoretical Physics. Meanwhile, he teamed up with Penrose to continue his study of singularities. His essay "Singularities and the Geometry of Space-Time" won the 1966 Adams Prize, which he shared with Penrose. The two continued to work together.

After completing their studies of the beginning of the universe, Hawking and Penrose turned to a prediction of its end, an event they called the Big Crunch. They proposed that gravity would eventually stop the expansion of the universe and ultimately overcome it. The universe would then contract to infinite density and eventually end in another singularity. Hawking worked out equations proving the theory. He was the first scientist to use both quantum mechanics, which studies objects smaller than atoms, and general relativity, which covers very large bodies, such as collapsed stars.

The year 1967 was a good one for Hawking. On May 28, 1967, his son Robert was born. Later that fall, his fellowship was extended for two more years, which meant Hawking and Penrose could continue to pursue their research. In 1968, their joint essay, "On

INTERESTING FACTS ABOUT BLACK HOLES

- American astronomer John Wheeler got tired of saying "gravitationally collapsed stars" to describe the increasing density of dying stars. In 1967, he coined the term "black hole" and got the attention of the popular press.
- Einstein's theory of relativity predicted the existence of black holes in 1916.
- The first real-life black hole—an invisible body ten times the mass of Earth's sun—was discovered in the Cygnus constellation in December 1970.
- Gravity attracts particles into a black hole but does not suck them in like a vacuum cleaner. Instead, matter "falls" into it.
- No one could drop into a black hole and survive. The body would stretch out like a very long, thin noodle.
- Estimates of the number of black holes in the Milky Way range from ten million to one billion.
- Scientists have identified a sound emanating from the radioactive fallout from a black hole in the Perseus constellation two hundred fifty million light years from Earth as B-flat, fifty-seven octaves below middle C. The noise is one million billion times lower than the lowest sound the human ear can detect.

Gravitational Collapse and Cosmology," won second prize in the Gravity Research Foundation Awards. Hawking's reputation as a scientist grew.

Hawking next collaborated with George Ellis to further study Penrose's ideas and write a book based on the Adams Prize essay. *The Large Scale Structure of Space-Time* was published in 1973. The highly technical book was nearly impossible to read, even for many scientists. However, it later became a classic physics textbook.

With his renewed fellowship scheduled to end, Hawking needed a new job. His trouble speaking had worsened, and he found that he could no longer teach. Some friends at Cambridge spread a rumor that Kings College would soon offer Hawking a senior research fellowship, causing officials at Gonville and Caius College to offer him a six-year special Fellowship for Distinction in Science.

On November 2, 1969, Hawking's daughter, Lucy, was born. Hawking's physical condition continued to deteriorate. Only his closest friends could understand his speech. He could no longer walk with a cane and traded it in for a wheelchair. Regardless, he and Penrose extended their research. Hawking's thesis had shown that the universe began as an exploding singularity. With Penrose he further showed that the Big Bang was the only way space and time could have begun. Hawking saw the entire universe as a huge black hole turned inside out.

Illustration of a supermassive black hole, showing the center surrounded by a disk of dust and gas attracted by gravity. Hawking is a pioneer in black-hole theory.

A few days after Lucy's birth, an idea popped into Hawking's head as he got into bed. In what Hawking called a "Eureka moment" on his Web site, he realized he could apply the theory he developed for singularities to black holes, thus changing his research focus. He had already studied a black hole's interior. Now he looked at the point where a black hole began. That point—the distance where light can no longer resist a black hole's gravitation—is known as its event horizon. In short, it's the black hole's edge. Hawking set out to prove that the event horizon remained constant.

CHAPTER FOUR

ON THE HORIZON

While Hawking worked, a Princeton University graduate student named Jacob Bekenstein was working on the idea that the size of the event horizon would break down and be subject to disorder. At first, Hawking disagreed. He said that for that to be true, a black hole would have to radiate energy, but that couldn't happen if nothing could escape the hole's heavy-duty gravity.

Hawking went to Moscow in what was then the Soviet Union to consult with two Russian physicists, Yakov Zeldovich and Alexander Starobinsky, who were also working on the problem. They maintained that a black hole could emit particles. Hawking, though, questioned their calculations. He returned to Cambridge and worked on the mathematics of the problem.

"ABSOLUTE RUBBISH!"

In the course of his calculations and research, Hawking discovered that he had been wrong. Not only could the edge of a black hole decrease, but in theory, the entire black hole itself could lose mass and energy and completely disappear. As that happened, its temperature would increase, and it would emit more and more radiation. At a critical point before the hole disintegrated, it would explode with the force of millions of hydrogen bombs.

He took his research to Dennis Sciama, his postgraduate adviser, who shared Hawking's excitement and told other scientists about his student's ideas. Soon after that, Hawking presented a talk titled "Black Hole Explosions?" at the Second Quantum Gravity Conference. The audience sat stunned as Hawking presented a bold theory that defied convention. John G. Taylor, a professor from the University of London who moderated Hawking's session, rose and shouted, "Sorry, Stephen, but this is absolute rubbish!"

While some scientists doubted Hawking's new theory, others were enthusiastic. They checked and double-checked Hawking's calculations, and they held up. Eventually,

Perhaps a future space probe will study a black hole and Hawking radiation, represented by the blue glow in this illustration. Even though light cannot escape a black hole, some radioactive particles may get away.

even Professor Taylor agreed. Hawking was right again. As his theory gained acceptance, the particles that left black holes as they disintegrate became known as "Hawking radiation."

The respected scientific journal *Nature* published "Black Hole Explosions?" in 1974. Hawking's reputation soared. He was just thirty-two years of age when the Royal Society invited him to become one of their youngest members ever.

A STELLAR YEAR

In 1979, the Hawking family added a new member. A second son, Timothy, was born on Easter Sunday. By this time, Hawking's ALS had progressed so that he needed constant nursing attention.

In this 1981 family photo, Hawking holds his son Tim on his lap and is flanked by *(left to right)* daughter Lucy, son Robert, and his wife, Jane, outside their home in Cambridge.

In the 1600s, the Roman Catholic Church persecuted Galileo for his revolutionary ideas about the universe. In 1979, the Church praised Hawking for his. Hawking's work on the Big Bang agreed with the Church's belief that God created the heavens and Earth. Hawking received the Pope Pius XI Gold Medal for Science.

In November, Cambridge University bestowed another honor. University officials named Hawking the Lucasian Professor of Mathematics at Cambridge's Department of Applied Mathematics and Theoretical Physics. Many esteemed scientists have been named to the professorship, including Sir Isaac Newton, who held the post in 1669. (Hawking resigned the professorship thirty years later when he retired in 2009.)

Hawking revisited his thoughts about the Big Bang and began to

Cambridge student Chris Hull consults with Hawking about theoretical physics in 1985, before a major health setback temporarily put the professor on the sidelines.

refine his ideas. He considered the possibility that the universe may have begun in a very small space, but not as infinitely small as a singularity. Perhaps a continuous cycle of Big Bangs, followed by Big Crunches, exploded and condensed repeatedly before the universe reached a point of creation. The universe, then, would have no starting point, no real beginning. This idea is known as the "no boundary proposal," which no longer required the hand of God to start things off.

However, the question of why the universe exists at all remained. Hawking, who describes himself as a principled atheist, has been quoted as saying, "If you like, you can define God to be the answer to that question."

AWARDS AND HONORS

Stephen Hawking has received a number of awards and honors during his career, including the following:

- 1975 Eddington Medal from the Royal Astronomical Society
- 1976 Hughes Medal from the Royal Society of London

- 1976 Dannie Heineman Prize for Mathematical Physics from the American Physical Society
- 1985 Gold Medal from the Royal Astronomical Society
- 1987 Paul Dirac Medal from the Institute of Physics
- 1989 Physics Prize from the Wolf Foundation for work on black holes (shared with Roger Penrose)
- 1999 Julius Edgar Lilienfeld Prize from the American Physical Society
- 2005 James Smithson Bicentennial Medal from the Smithsonian Institution
- 2006 Copley Medal from the Royal Society of London
- 2009 U.S. Presidential Medal of Freedom

Additionally, his written work has also received professional recognition:

- The essay "Singularities and the Geometry of Space-Time" wins Adams Prize (1966)
- The essay "On Gravitational Collapse and Cosmology," co-authored by Robert Penrose, wins second prize in the Gravity Research Foundation Award (1968)
- The essay "Black Holes" wins the Gravity Research Foundation Award (1971)
- *The Universe in a Nutshell* wins Aventis Book Prize for excellence in popular science writing (2002)

THE STORY OF SPACE AND TIME

The scientific inquiry into the origins of the universe stirred in Hawking a desire to explain cosmology to those who had little or no science background. Also, he needed money for his children's education and for his own health care. His friend Simon Mitton, a radio astronomer, suggested he write a book for readers outside the scientific community. Hawking agreed. He wanted to write a best seller—the kind of book sold in airports and grocery stores.

He started the manuscript that became *A Brief History of Time*. Mitton was concerned that early drafts were too technical. For example, an equation appeared on nearly every page. Hawking tried to simplify the writing while discussing the history of science, the expanding universe, Einstein's theory of general relativity, his own work on black holes, and the possibility that there was an overriding "theory of everything"—a way to explain the entire universe. The task was far from easy.

A literary agent presented the book to publishers in the United States. Several expressed interest, in particular W. W. Norton & Co., which was known for publishing books for elite readers, and Bantam Books, which published popular books for the mass market. Hawking's decision was easy; he signed with

Bantam. Despite the scientist's efforts to describe technical science to nontechnical readers in a simplified version, his editor at Bantam wanted an even more readable book. He also asked Hawking to explain basic concepts that the author had assumed his potential readers already knew. Hawking worked on another rewrite.

A BIG SETBACK

In 1985, Hawking and his family planned to spend the summer in Geneva. Hawking wanted to visit a particle accelerator facility there while the rest of the family vacationed. Hawking got there first, along with his private nurse, Laura Gentry. One night when Gentry checked on Hawking, she found him gasping for breath, and his skin had turned purple from lack of oxygen.

She rushed him to a hospital, where doctors put him on a ventilator and put him into a drug-induced coma. Hawking had pneumonia, a lung disease that often kills people with ALS. When Jane Hawking arrived, doctors asked if she wanted them to remove life support and let her husband die.

The alternative was a tracheotomy, a surgical procedure where a doctor cuts an opening in the windpipe and inserts a tube, which lets air reach the lungs. The procedure would eliminate the coughing that often disrupted Hawking's breath-ing, but it meant that he would never speak again. Jane Hawking insisted that her husband must live, and doctors performed the tracheotomy.

Soon after Hawking's recovery from the life-threatening experi-ence, he received an exciting gift. Walt Woltosz, a California computer expert, had designed a computer program that he called the Equalizer. The program came loaded with nearly three thousand selected words, which, when selected onscreen, were processed through a synthesizer. In other words, the Equalizer allowed Hawking to speak despite the tracheotomy. For Hawking's use, the program's vocabulary list included many scientific words. The only draw-back was that the voice had an American accent. Hawking would have preferred a voice with British inflections. To accommodate Hawking's medical condition, one of his students designed a switch

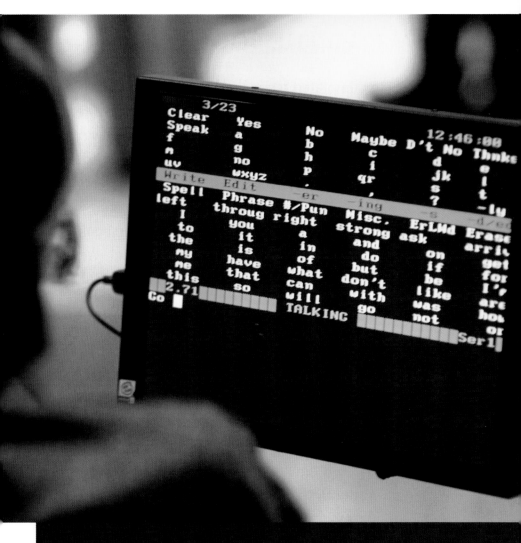

An image showing Equalizer software at work. Hawking is able to communicate using the software, which allows him to select words that are then transferred to a speech synthesizer.

that would operate the program. Slight squeezing, which Hawking could still manage, or simple head or eye movement activated the switch.

BACK TO THE BOOK

Hawking completed his manuscript, and Bantam released *A Brief History of Time* in 1988. The reviews were positive. A reviewer at the *New York Review of Books* wrote, "[Hawking] can explain the complexities of cosmological physics with an engaging combination of clarity and wit." Another reviewer, working for the *Sunday Times* in London, wrote, "This book marries a child's wonder to a genius's intellect. We journey into Hawking's universe while marveling at his mind." The *Wall Street Journal* simply called the book "masterful," while the *New York Times* declared, "Mr. Hawking clearly possesses a natural teacher's gifts—easy, good-natured humor and an ability to illustrate highly complex propositions with analogies plucked from daily life."

The book soared to the top of best-seller lists in the United Kingdom and the United States. It stayed on the British *Sunday Times* best-seller list for an impressive 237 weeks—which, according to Hawking's Web site, also landed the book a spot in the *Guinness Book of World Records*. It stayed on the *New York Times* best-seller list for more than a year. *A Brief History of Time* has sold more than two hundred million copies in more than three dozen languages, according to Kristine Larsen, author of *Stephen Hawking: A Biography*.

Writings by and about Hawking, on display at the Science Museum of London to commemorate Hawking's seventieth birthday, in 2012.

The book's last line became known worldwide. Hawking had referred to the possibility of a theory of everything, which could eventually inform a discussion of why the universe exists. He ended the book with, "If we find the answer to that, it would be the ultimate triumph of human reason—for then we would know the mind of God."

STARSTRUCK

Hawking became an instant celebrity. During his travels and daily activities, people recognized him on the

CELEBRITY STATUS

The skyrocketing success of *A Brief History of Time* propelled Hawking to stardom. Over the years he has enjoyed playing with his celebrity status by appearing in a variety of popular venues.

- In 1983, Hawking made a guest appearance on the television show *Star Trek: The Next Generation*, playing himself as a hologram.
- Pink Floyd featured Hawking's synthesized voice in the 1994 song "Keep Talking."
- Hawking appeared as a guest on the interview show *Larry King Live* in 1999.
- Hawking performed a voice-over for a 1999 episode of *The Simpsons*. He returned to the show for an encore in 2005.
- Hawking appeared in a brief skit with Jim Carrey on a 2003 broadcast of *Late Night with Conan O'Brien*.
- Hawking played himself in the 2009 movie *Beyond the Horizon*, about a reporter working on a story about cosmology.

street. The press compared him to Albert Einstein, and *People* magazine named him one of the Twenty-Five Most Interesting People of 1988. To Hawking's delight, Berke Breathed, author of the popular comic strip *Bloom County*, fashioned a race between his child-genius character and Hawking to see who could come up with the theory of everything first. Owners of the Gold Star Sardine Bar in Chicago decided Hawking needed a fan club to honor a "real hero." They ordered Stephen Hawking Fan Club T-shirts and gave away more than eight thousand of them in just two months.

Susan Anderson *(seated, center)*, cofounder of the Stephen Hawking Fan Club at the Gold Star Sardine Bar in Chicago. The bar gave away T-shirts to celebrate Hawking's accomplishments.

In the United Kingdom, Hawking received an honorary doctorate in science from Cambridge University, presented by the Duke of Edinburgh. Later, Queen Elizabeth honored Hawking with a Companion of Honour title, a rank higher than Sir Isaac Newton's rank of knighthood. Hawking also won a Britannica Award for being a "supreme communicator to lay readers of extremely difficult physical concepts."

The pressure of celebrity affected the entire Hawking family. Their daily lives were fraught with interruptions, and their personal interactions with each other suffered as well. Although Hawking refused to discuss the reasons, he and Jane officially separated in 1990, just a few months before their twenty-fifth wedding anniversary.

UNIVERSAL QUESTIONS

Media interviews, consultations with international physicists, travel to lecture all over the world, and bags upon bags of mail to be answered gave Hawking little time for science, yet he persevered in his work. Shortly before the publication of *A Brief History of Time*, Hawking had turned his attention to a new question: what happens to matter that falls into a black hole?

He thought the particles might travel through a wormhole—or space tunnel—to another place and time in the universe or to an independent, closed universe he called a baby universe. This theory depended on the use of imaginary time, a concept Hawking explained in *A Brief History of Time*. No less real than regular time, which runs from the past through the present to the future, imaginary time runs perpendicular to the regular timeline. In imaginary time no distinction exists between time and

65

space. Imaginary time is an accepted mathematical concept that Hawking applied to cosmology.

MORE TO SAY

Hawking's next book was a collection of essays for the mass market titled *Black Holes and Baby Universes and Other Essays*, published in 1993. The thirteen essays built on Hawking's first book. In the collection, he further discussed imaginary time, how baby universes can form out of black holes, the chances of a black hole existing at the center of the Milky Way, and the search for a unified theory that explained everything in the universe. The book also revealed parts of Hawking's personal life. He wrote about his experience battling ALS, and in one essay listed the eight records he would want to have if he were stranded on a desert island.

This time reviews were less glowing than those for *A Brief History of Time*. In *Library Journal*, reviewer Gregg Sapp called *Black Holes and Baby Universes and Other Essays* "unbalanced." He wrote, "The biographical pieces are digressive and not particularly enlightening … The scientific essays are much stronger and offer insight into a variety of cutting-edge issues in contemporary physics."

The *New York Times* review was more positive. "[Hawking] sprinkles his explanations with a wry sense of humor and a keen awareness that the sciences today delve not only into the far reaches of the cosmos, but into the inner philosophical world as well."

The public, however, loved the book, which was even easier to understand than *A Brief History of Time*, and the writing was compelling. As before, the book hit best-seller lists around the world.

TRAVELING IN STYLE AND TIME

In 1995, Hawking and his wife Jane officially divorced; later that year he married his nurse and travelling companion Elaine Mason. Hawking stayed on the go, delivering lectures, appearing on television shows and in movies, and consulting with other physicists. Because of his frequent trips, he needed a stronger wheelchair so that he could travel in style.

Hawking married his second wife, Elaine Mason, at the register office at Shire Hall in Cambridge on September 15, 1995.

An American couple, Mike and Terri Rozaieski, designed one for him and called it the Quantum Jazzy

HELPING OTHERS WITH DISABILITIES

While Stephen Hawking seemed to get his interest in science from his father, it was his mother who led by example when it came to social issues. Perhaps the issue closest to his heart was disability rights.

Hawking has been at the forefront of a number of measures aimed at helping people with disabilities. Thanks in part to public awareness of his medical situation, the Cambridge City Council approved ramps in public buildings, curb cuts, and accessible polling places. Hawking also helped raise funds for living quarters for students with disabilities at Cambridge and Bristol Universities. The dormitory in Bristol, England, was named "Hawking House" in appreciation.

In 1999, Hawking joined Bishop Desmond Tutu and dignitaries from China, Russia, Saudi Arabia, and other countries in signing the Charter for the Third Millennium on Disability. The document calls upon governments worldwide to work toward preventing conditions and illness that cause disabilities. The World Health assembly of Rehabilitation International in London adopted the charter, spurring the organization's president, Arthur O'Reilly, to call for a United Nations convention on the rights of people with disabilities.

"It is no use complaining about the public's attitude about the disabled," Hawking said in a speech at the University of Southern California in 1990. "It is up to disabled people to change people's awareness in the same way that blacks and women have changed public perceptions."

1400 Power Chair. Terri, who also used a wheelchair, was pregnant with her first child, and Hawking talked with her about being a parent with a disability. He is quoted as telling her, "It might seem awkward being a disabled parent, but I did not find it so. Children accept as natural that you are in a wheelchair. Ask for their help. Don't worry. Just make them part of the family team."

Hawking took his new wheelchair to Germany for the launch of his next book, *The Universe in a Nutshell*. Written for a popular audience, the book further expounded on material from *A Brief History of Time*. It discussed those topics in more depth and added new ones. Also in the book was a discussion of the possibility of time travel. Hawking wrote, "Time travel is indeed taking place on a microscopic level." However, later in the book he added, "The laws of physics conspire to prevent time travel by

In the best-selling *The Universe in a Nutshell*, Hawking discussed the possibility of time travel, multiple universes, and dark matter in a way that the general public could understand.

macroscopic objects," like humans. Hawking also discounted conspiracy theories regarding UFOs traveling to Earth from the future and the accompanying government cover-up.

In a *School Library Journal* review of *Nutshell*, Christine C. Menefee wrote:

> Writing in a lighthearted, personal, often humorous style and with colorful and entertaining graphics on every page, Hawking succeeds in communicating his love and enthusiasm for science. Without seeming to condescend, he makes a valiant attempt to clarify many fascinating and elusive topics such as relativity and time; multiple universes and dimensions; black holes and dark matter; prediction of the future; and the possibility of time travel.

EXPLANATIONS AND SIMPLIFICATIONS

In 2002, Running Press published another mass-market volume by Hawking. *On the Shoulders of Giants*, which Hawking edited, showed how classic works about great discoveries in physics and astronomy, made by the likes of Nicolaus Copernicus, Galileo Galilei, Johannes Kepler, Sir Isaac Newton, and Albert Einstein, changed the world. The book followed the evolution of modern science and included commentary by Hawking.

A critic from *Booklist* noted that readers would need a degree of "mathematical ability" to understand the work. But *Publishers Weekly* praised it, stating, "Acclaimed physicist Hawking has collected in this single illuminating volume the classic works of physics and astronomy that in their day revolutionized humankind's perception of the world ... Hawking has given these works a setting that is elegantly simple and, in its simplicity, effectively broadening."

While furthering his research, Hawking began rethinking his first book for non-scientists. Despite all the work and revision it took to make *A Brief History of Time* readable and understandable to the general public, he decided it was still too complicated. He began a collaboration with Leonard Mlodinow, a physicist at the California Institute of Technology in Pasadena and a screenwriter for such television series as *Star Trek: The Next Generation.* They revised the original work and published *A Briefer History of Time* in 2005.

The reconceived book explained such key concepts as space and time, the role of God in creation, and the past and future of the universe, exceeding its predecessor by including the latest developments in the field. One such advance was string theory, an idea that the building blocks of the physical world are one-dimensional strings, not the particles without dimensions that had formed the basis of early physics. *Publishers Weekly* "highly recommended" *A Briefer History*, stating, "Hawking and Mlodinow provide one of the most lucid discussions of [string theory] ever written for a general audience."

Hawking's book *God Created the Integers: The Mathematical Breakthroughs That Changed History* was also released by Running Press in 2005. Like *On the Shoulders of Giants*, this book was an anthology edited by Hawking. It included excerpts of the work of fifteen mathematicians on twenty-five landmark "masterpieces" of mathematical writing. The book included brief biographies of the writers, along with explanations of the significance of their work.

God Created the Integers is not for those with a mathematics phobia. In her review for Amazon.com, Therese Littleton wrote, "Dense with numbers, formulae, and ideas, *God Created the Integers* is quite challenging, but Hawking rewards curious readers with a look at how mathematics has been built."

It was during this period that Hawking found it necessary to make an adjustment in how he communicated with the world. For years he had been controlling his computer by gently pressing a button. However, he lost the use of the muscles in his hand that made that happen. In 2005, he switched to an infrared device in his eyeglasses that detected slight movements in his cheek and translated them into word choices for his synthesized voice unit.

Something else also disrupted Hawking's busy work schedule. He and his second wife, Elaine, filed for divorce in late 2006.

FLY ME TO THE MOON

Always up for a challenge, Hawking announced that his next goal was to travel into space. The next year, in preparation for a space flight with Richard Branson's Virgin Galactic company, Hawking took a zero-gravity flight aboard a modified Boeing 727. The jet, owned by the U.S. corporation Zero Gravity, had a padded interior to protect passengers during the experience. For Hawking's trip, the firm waived the $3,750 fare it charges other passengers.

Hawking experiencing zero gravity in 2007, preparing for a planned trip into space.

The aircraft took off from the Kennedy Space Center in Florida on April 26, 2007. The jet climbed at a sharp angle, then plunged, repeating the maneuver eight times. The motions created a feeling of weightlessness. Hawking, without his wheelchair, was weightless for a total of about four minutes. In an interview with BBC News, Hawking said, "It was amazing! The zero-G part was wonderful ... I could have gone on forever. Space, here I come!"

Hawking made a reservation for a suborbital flight on a Virgin Galactic commercial trip to space. He is one of five hundred passengers, including actor Ashton Kutcher, who have already booked flights. Virgin Galactic completed the first rocket-powered flight of its space vehicle *SpaceShipTwo* on April 29, 2013. The flight was the first of the final phase of testing before full operations could begin. The "spaceline" hoped to begin commercial flights from Spaceport America in New Mexico by the end of the year.

COLLABORATION, COMPILATION, AND CONSCIOUSNESS

CHAPTER SIX

A long with writing popular books, preparing for space flight, and giving lectures, Hawking continued to research and write for a scientific audience. He often collaborated with James B. Hartle, research professor of physics at the University of California, Santa Barbara, with whom he had worked in the early 1980s.

In their 1983 paper "Wave Function of the Universe," published in *Physical Review*, Hawking and Hartle proposed that the universe is finite but did not begin with a singularity. Instead, they proposed that the universe was like a particle, thereby combining the study of the very small with that of the very large. The paper met with controversy in the scientific world, yet it proved influential in urging further research.

Hawking also worked with Thomas Hertog, who, at the time of their collaboration, was a research associate at a government research agency in Paris. Hertog went on to become a professor of theoretical physics at the University of Leuven in Flanders, Belgium, in 2011. Hawking and Hertog proposed a way to test predictions about the nature of the universe and determine the properties of dark energy.

Hawking, Hartle, and Hertog co-authored several other academic articles and papers, including a trio of works on one subject: "No-Boundary Measure of the Universe" in 2007, "The Classical Universes of the No-Boundary Quantum State" in 2008, and "The

An artist's depiction of the universe. As Hawking had theorized, scientific evidence has shown that a supermassive black hole lies at the center of the Milky Way.

No-Boundary Measure in the Regime of Eternal Inflation" in 2010. The three also authored "Local Observation in Eternal Inflation," "Accelerated Expansion from Negative Lambda," and "Inflation with Negative Lambda," between 2011 and 2012.

BOOKS FOR KIDS

Hawking also teamed up with other authors while writing new books for the mass market. Likely closest to his heart were the children's books for readers in grades three through seven that he co-authored with his daughter, Lucy. Simon & Schuster Books for Young Readers published *George's Secret Key to the Universe* in 2007. The book follows a boy named George on a trip through space, where he encounters, among other things, Hawking radiation.

Like Hawking's books for adults, *George's Secret Key to the Universe* was well received. The *Bookseller* called it "gripping, informative and funny," while *Junior* magazine wrote that the book was "a roller-coaster ride." The [London] *Sunday Times* reviewer wrote, "It makes a case for the relevance and fascination of physics, and for the importance of scientists and eco-warriors working together to save the planet." *George's Secret Key to the Universe* was a *New York Times* best seller and was selected for Al's Book Club on the television show *Today*.

Lucy Hawking, holding a copy of a book she co-wrote with her father. *George's Secret Key to the Universe* was the first in a series they wrote.

The father-daughter team published *George's Cosmic Treasure Hunt*, another book in what turned out to be a series, in 2009. This time George was involved in a galactic treasure hunt wherein he had to crack a secret code to prevent Earth's destruction.

As research for the book, Lucy Hawking got to take a zero-gravity flight, like her father. She also interviewed astronauts at Cape Kennedy and the Johnson Space Center, which added a sense of authenticity to the fictional account. Reviews were lukewarm. In the *School Library Journal*, Walter Minkel wrote, "If not spellbinding, [*George's Cosmic Treasure Hunt*] will please fans of the first book. Fun cartoon drawings throughout carry along the unsubtle tale whose message seems to be 'Wow! Isn't science great?'"

A third book in the series for young readers came out in 2012. In *George and the Big Bang*, George travels to Switzerland for an important experiment, hoping to discover how the universe began, only to receive a mysterious message revealing that someone plans to ruin the experiment. A graphic novel at the end of the book explains the Big Bang.

DESIGNING MEN (OF SCIENCE)

In the same period when he was writing with his daughter, Hawking also worked with Leonard

Mlodinow on their second book for adult readers. Bantam Books released *The Grand Design*, which contemplates the universe's existence and the laws of physics, in 2010.

Hawking explained his purpose for writing the book on Amazon.com: *"A Brief History of Time* left some important questions unanswered. Why is there a universe—why is there something rather than nothing? Why do we exist? Why are the laws of nature what they are? Did the universe need a designer and creator?" He added that he and his co-author had tried to answer the "ultimate question of life, the universe, and everything":

> In *The Grand Design* we explain why, according to quantum theory, the cosmos does not have just a single existence, or history, but rather that every possible history of the universe exists simultaneously. We question the conventional concept of reality, posing instead a 'model-dependent' theory of reality. We discuss how the laws of our particular universe are extraordinarily finely tuned so as to allow for our existence, and show why quantum theory predicts the multiverse—the idea that ours is just one of many universes

that appeared spontaneously out of nothing, each with different laws of nature.

Acknowledging the complicated nature of the material, *Publishers Weekly* wrote, in part, "Even general readers will be able to follow along as the authors guide us through ... mind-blowing cosmological discoveries of the last century."

DREAMING

In 2011, Running Press published a third anthology edited by Hawking. Like the two previous books, *The Dreams That Stuff Is Made Of: The Most Astounding Papers on Quantum Physics—and How They Shook the Scientific World* brought together important writings by scientists, this time featuring scientists who had studied the atom. Contributors included Max Planck, Albert Einstein, Niels Bohr, and Richard Feynman.

The *Times Higher Education Supplement* wrote, "Experts will relish these paradigm-shifting concepts...physicists will find it a joy. For them the title is well chosen." Other reviews sought to encourage less science-savvy readers. *Publishers Weekly* gave the book a starred review, noting, "Even those with a minimal background in math and science will come away with a keen understanding of the towering genius and his transformative work on the nature of space, time, and light."

In a back-handed compliment *New Scientist* said, "Novice readers will be surprised at how readable much of it is." But a reviewer for *CHOICE: Current Reviews for Academic Libraries*, recommended it for upper-division undergraduates and above, allowing that the book was worth reading due to "Hawking's very clear, concise introductions to each chapter."

The reviews served to feed Hawking's reputation as one of the world's greatest scientists. Again he used his platform to weigh in on global issues.

HAWKING BOYCOTTS ISRAEL

Hawking was scheduled to speak at the fifth annual Israeli Presidential Conference "Facing Tomorrow 2013" in Jerusalem. The conference was to focus on developments that would shape Israel's future. Although Hawking had originally accepted the invitation to speak, and had in fact visited the country a handful of times before, he later changed his mind and joined an academic and cultural boycott of Israel organized by the British Committee for the Universities of Palestine. According to the

Israeli prime minister Ehud Olmert meets with Hawking in 2006. Three years later, Hawking declined a speaking engagement in Israel because of an academic boycott.

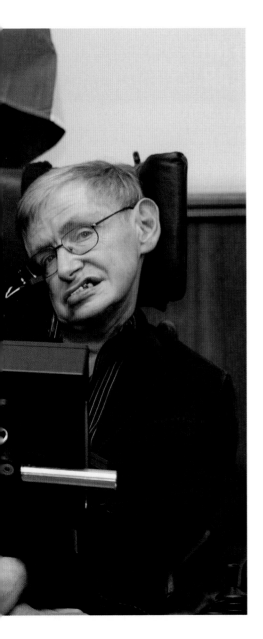

group's Web site, the purpose of the boycott was to oppose the Israeli occupation of Palestinian lands and Israel's "persistent suppression of Palestinian academic freedom."

Cambridge University issued a statement reported in the *New York Times* that Hawking's withdrawal from the high-profile event was "based on advice from Palestinian academics that he should respect the boycott." In the same article Yigal Palmor, spokesperson for Israel's Foreign Ministry, was quoted as saying, "Never has a scientist of this stature boycotted Israel."

THE END IS NEAR

Hawking was not shy about standing up for what he believed was right. In 2007, he delivered the keynote address at an event held to move the Doomsday Clock closer to midnight. The Doomsday Clock is a symbol used by the *Bulletin of the Atomic Scientists* at the University of Chicago to warn of such man-made threats to human civilization as nuclear holocaust and climate change. Earth's destruction is symbolized by midnight on the clock. Hawking serves on the organization's board of sponsors.

The Doomsday Clock was set at seven minutes to midnight in 1947. The bulletin had moved it eighteen times as of 2007. In 1953, after the United States tested the hydro-gen bomb, the time on the clock

Hawking during a 2007 press conference on the "Doomsday Clock," which symbolizes the risk of catastrophic events caused or influenced by human activity.

moved to two minutes to midnight. When the Soviet Union collapsed in 1991, the minute hand moved back to 11:43 PM. In 2007, the time was changed to 11:55 PM

The 2007 event marked the first time that the clock moved closer to midnight due to climate change. Hawking has said global warming posed a greater threat to Earth than terrorism. As reported in *USA Today*, he said, "Terror only kills hundreds or thousands of people. Global warming could kill millions. We should have a war on global warming rather than the war on terror."

SILENCED GENIUS?

Through all this, Hawking's physical condition worsened. For years he had twitched the facial muscles in his cheek to trigger a tiny infrared sensor on his glasses. The sensor then told his computer which words were to be spoken by his now well-known synthesized voice. However, those cheek muscles had grown weaker.

When Hawking started using the system, he could communicate at about fifteen words per minute. By 2012, however, he was down to just one. Composing one or two paragraphs of text could take an hour.

Researchers at Intel Corporation, which has worked with Hawking's computer system since the late 1990s, worked to solve the problem. In late summer 2013, the company offered hope. Justin Rattner, Intel's chief technology officer and director of Intel Labs, said Hawking could make several facial expressions other than twitching his cheek, including movement of his mouth and eyebrow. Intel then went to work on a system that could take advantage of those movements to signal Hawking's computer. Researchers at the company were also considering the use of facial-recognition software that would help Hawking communicate faster than by selecting individual letters or words.

LOOKING UP

Another book by Hawking was published by Bantam Books in September 2013. This time, instead of explaining the universe, Hawking explained himself. In *My Brief History*, Hawking took readers from his childhood, through his struggles with ALS, to his triumphant career in science.

Sally Gaminara, publishing director at Bantam, told the [London] *Telegraph*, "As publishers of Stephen Hawking's iconic *A Brief History of Time* in 1988 and all his subsequent titles, we are delighted to be able to publish his memoir twenty-five years later. It is a remarkable testimony to his courage and tenacity that we can do so."

So what's next for the world's greatest cosmologist? He still wants to travel in space. If his past resolve is any indication, he will surely do whatever it takes to get there. If he makes it, he will be among the first

Hawking and his daughter, Lucy, presenting during the National Aeronautics and Space Administration fiftieth anniversary celebration in 2008. Hawking is a proponent of space travel.

civilian space tourists. And if he was right in a 2001 interview reported in the *Telegraph*, many more people will follow.

In the interview with the *Telegraph*, Hawking commented, "I don't think the human race will survive the next thousand years, unless we spread into space. There are too many accidents that can befall life on a single planet. But I'm an optimist. We will reach out to the stars."

TIMELINE

1942 Stephen Hawking is born on January 8 in Cambridge, England.

1959 Hawking enters the University of Oxford.

1962 Hawking develops "troubling symptoms," including clumsiness and is diagnosed with ALS. He enters Cambridge University.

1965 Hawking marries Jane Wilde on July 14.

1966 Hawking earns doctorate from Cambridge.

1967 Hawking's first child, Robert, is born on May 28.

1970 Hawking's daughter, Lucy, is born on November 2.

1973 Hawking co-authors *The Large Scale Structure of Space-Time* with George Ellis.

1974 Hawking is inducted into the Royal Society.

1977 Hawking receives rank of professor of gravitational physics.

1979 Hawking's son Timothy is born on Easter Sunday.

1982 Hawking is invested as a Commander of the British Empire.

1986 Hawking's father, Frank Hawking, dies after a long illness. Hawking is appointed to the Pontifical Academy of Sciences.

1988 Hawking's first book for popular audiences, *A Brief History of Time*, is published by Bantam Books.

1989 Hawking receives honorary doctorate in science from the University of Cambridge. Queen Elizabeth II presents Hawking the Companion of Honour medal.

1992 Hawking's *Brief History of Time* premiers in a movie version.

1993 Hawking publishes *Black Holes and Baby Universes.*

1995 Hawking divorces Jane and marries Elaine Mason.

1996 Hawking's book *The Illustrated A Brief History of Time* is released.

2002 Hawking publishes *The Universe in a Nutshell.*

2005 Hawking begins using an infrared device controlled by his facial muscles to operate his computer. Hawking and co-author Leonard Mlodinow publish *A Briefer History of Time.*

2006 Hawking and wife Elaine file for divorce. Hawking announces desire to go into space.

2007 Hawking takes a zero-gravity flight to prepare for space travel and makes a reservation for a commercial trip to space aboard Virgin Galactic "spaceline." Hawking publishes *God Created the Integers.* Hawking and his daughter, Lucy, publish *George's Secret Key to the Universe.* Hawking speaks at an event to set the Doomsday Clock to 11:58 PM. because of the threat of global warming.

2009 Hawking and his daughter publish *George's Cosmic Treasure.*

2010 Hawking and Leonard Mlodinow publish *The Grand Design.*

2011 Hawking's anthology *The Dreams That Stuff Is Made Of: The Most Astounding Papers on Quantum Physics—and How They Shook the Scientific World* is published.

2012 Hawking and his daughter publish *George and the Big Bang.*

2013 Hawking joins an academic and cultural boycott of Israel to support Palestinian causes and withdraws from the "Facing Tomorrow 2013" conference in Jerusalem. Hawking's autobiography *My Brief Story* is published.

GLOSSARY

baby universe A closed, independent universe outside our own.

Big Bang The explosion that created the universe and the beginning of time.

Big Crunch A theoretical event that happens when the universe collapses into itself to almost infinite density.

cosmology A branch of astronomy that studies the universe and its past, present, and future.

dissertation A lengthy written treatment of a subject; a thesis, especially one submitted for a doctorate.

Doomsday Clock A symbol used to illustrate the danger of such man-made threats to Earth as nuclear holocaust and climate change.

event horizon The distance where light can no longer resist a black hole's gravitation.

fellowship A paid research position in a college or university. The fellow gets a place to study in return for teaching.

general relativity A description of space and time based on Albert Einstein's geometric theory of gravitation.

Hawking radiation Particles that radiate from black holes as they disintegrate.

memoir A literary book or essay that gives a personal account of one's life experiences; an autobiography.

metaphysics The study of reality beyond what can be determined through the five senses.

natural science One of the following disciplines of science: astronomy, biology, chemistry, Earth science, and physics.

prognosis A medical prediction of the future of a patient's illness or condition.

singularity A point of infinite density that exists when stars completely collapse.

space-time A four-dimensional system of coordinates that include three dimensions of space and one of time.

string theory The idea that the building blocks of the physical world are one-dimensional strings, not particles without dimensions.

wormhole A tunnel-like pathway between two regions of space and time or from one universe to another independent one.

FOR MORE INFORMATION

ALS Association, National Headquarters
1275 K Street NW, Suite 1050
Washington, DC 20005
(202) 407-8580
Web site: http://www.alsa.org
The ALS Association is a nonprofit organization that
fights Lou Gehrig's disease through research, care
services, and partnerships with government.

American Astronomical Society (AAS)
2000 Florida Avenue NW, Suite 400
Washington, DC 20009-1231
(202) 328-2010
Web site: https://aas.org
The AAS is an organization of professional astrono-
mers in North America. Its mission is to enhance
and share humanity's scientific understanding of
the universe.

American Institute of Mathematics
360 Portage Avenue
Palo Alto, CA 94306-2244
(650) 845-2071
Web site: http://www.aimath.org
The American Institute of Mathematics is a nonprofit
organization that supports mathematical research,

sponsors conferences, and develops an online mathematics library. It also helps preserve the history of mathematics through collection and preservation of rare mathematical books and documents.

Canadian Astronomical Society
343 Sylvia Street
Victoria, BC V8V 1C5
Canada
(301) 675 8957
Web site: http://casca.ca
The Canadian Astronomical Society is a society of
    professional astronomers that promotes research
    and education about the universe. It holds annual
    scientific meetings, plans scientific projects,
    supports members' activities, and shares informa-
    tion among members and others.

Canadian Institute for Theoretical Astrophysics (CITA)
University of Toronto
60 St. George Street
Toronto, ON M5S 3H8
Canada
(416) 978-6879
Web site: http://www.cita.utoronto.ca
The CITA is a nonprofit organization that helps mem-
    bers of the Canadian theoretical astrophysics

community interact. It also serves as an international center of excellence for theoretical studies in astrophysics.

Mathematical Association of America (MAA)
1529 18th Street NW
Washington, DC 20036-1358
(800) 741-9415
Web site: http://www.maa.org
The MAA is a nonprofit organization of more than twenty-thousand faculty, students, practitioners, and others who love math. Founded in 1894, it works to move the profession forward.

National Space and Aeronautics Administration (NASA)
Public Communications Office
NASA Headquarters
Suite 5K39
Washington, DC 20546-000
(202) 358-0000
Web site: http://www.nasa.gov
NASA is an agency of the U.S. government that conducts and funds research concerning space and space technology.

The Whole Person
3710 Main Street

Kansas City, MO 64111

(800) 878-3037

Web site: http://www.thewholeperson.org

The Whole Person is a private, nonprofit corporation that provides community-based services for people with disabilities.

WEB SITES

Due to the changing nature of Internet links, Rosen Publishing has developed an online list of Web sites related to the subject of this book. This site is updated regularly. Please use this link to access the list:

http://www.rosenlinks.com/GSW/Hawk

FOR FURTHER READING

Adams, Douglas. *The Hitchhiker's Guide to the Galaxy.* New York, NY: Harmony Books, 1994.

Carroll, Sean. *From Eternity to Here: The Quest for the Ultimate Theory of Time.* Oxford, England: Oneworld Publications, 2011.

Close, Frank. *The Infinity Puzzle.* New York, NY: Basic Books, 2011.

Close, Frank. *Particle Physics: A Very Short Introduction.* Oxford, England: Oxford University Press, 2004.

Farndon, John. *The Great Scientists from Euclid to Stephen Hawking.* London, England: Arcturus Publishing Limited, 2012.

Flitcroft, Ian. *Journey by Starlight: A Time Traveler's Guide to Life, the Universe, and Everything.* New York, NY: One Peace Books, 2013.

Foster, Alan Dean. *Star Trek into Darkness.* New York, NY: Gallery Books, 2013.

Haddix, Margaret Peterson. *Found.* New York, NY: Simon & Schuster Books for Young Readers, 2008.

Hawking, Stephen W. *A Brief History of Time.* New York, NY: Bantam Books, 1998.

Hawking, Stephen W. *The Universe in a Nutshell.* New York, NY: Bantam Books, 2001.

Hawking, Stephen W., and Leonard Mlodinow. *The Grand Design.* New York, NY: Bantam Books, 2010.

Holder, Rodney. *Big Bang, Big God: A Universe Designed for Life?* Oxford, England: Lion Hudson, 2013.

Lederman, Leon, and Dick Teresi. *The God Particle: If the Universe Is the Answer, What Is the Question?* New York, NY: Dell Publishing, 1993.

L'Engle, Madeleine. *A Wrinkle in Time.* New York, NY: Square Fish, 2012.

Lennox, John C. *God and Stephen Hawking: Whose Design Is It Anyway?* Oxford, England: Lion Hudson, 2010.

Mitton, Simon. *Fred Hoyle: A Life in Science.* Cambridge, England: Cambridge University Press, 2011.

Peterson, Carolyn Collins. *Astronomy 101: From the Sun and Moon to Wormholes and Warp Drive, Key Theories, Discoveries, and Facts About the Universe.* Avon, MA: Adams Media, 2013.

Pincock, Stephen, and Mark Frary. *The Origins of the Universe for Dummies.* West Sussex, England: John Wiley & Sons, 2007.

Sample, Ian. *Massive: The Missing Particle That Sparked the Greatest Hunt in Science.* New York, NY: Basic Books, 2010.

Steele, Philip. *World History Biographies: Galileo: The Genius Who Charted the Universe.* Washington, DC: National Geographic Children's Books, 2008.

BIBLIOGRAPHY

Bankston, John. *Stephen Hawking: Breaking the Boundaries of Space and Time.* Berkeley Heights, NJ: Enslow Publishers, 2005

Bardoe, Cheryl. "Stephen Hawking." *Ask*, Vol.10, No. 6, July/August 2011.

Cooper, Abraham. "Atheist Stephen Hawking and Church of Scotland Both Determined to Demonize Israel." FoxNews.com, May 9, 2013. Retrieved June 6, 2013 (http://foxnews.com/opinion/2013/05/09/atheist-stephen-hawking-and-church-scotland-both-determined-to-demonize-israel).

Dreifus, Claudia. "Life and the Cosmos, Word by Painstaking Word." *New York Times*, May 2011. Retrieved May 10, 2013 (http://www.nytimes.com/2011/05/10/science/10hawking.html?pagewanted=all&_r=0).

Farndon, John. *The Great Scientists*. London, England: Arcturus Publishing, 2010.

Fergusen, Kitty. *Stephen Hawking: An Unfettered Mind*. New York, NY: Palgrave Macmilan, 2012.

Folger, Tim. "Return of the Invisible Man." *Discover*, Vol. 30, No. 7, July/August 2009, pp. 42–91.

Hawking, Jane. *Music to Move the Stars: A Life with Stephen Hawking*. Philadelphia, PA: Trans-Atlantic Publications, 2000.

Hawking, Jane. *Travelling to Infinity: My Life with Stephen*. Richmond, Surrey, England: Alma Books., 2008.

Hawking, Lucy, and Stephen Hawking. "What Is a Black Hole?" *Ask*, Vol. 10, No. 6, July/August 2011, pp. 14–17.

Hawking, Stephen. "Brief Biography." Stephen Hawking Official Web site. Retrieved July 7, 2013 (http://www.hawking.org.uk/my-brief-history.html).

Hawking, Stephen. "Hawking at 70." *New Scientist*, Vol. 213, No. 2846, January 7, 2012, pp. 26–27.

Hawking, Stephen. "My Brief History." Stephen Hawking Official Web site. Retrieved July 7, 2013 (http://www.hawking.org.uk/about -stephen.html).

Kershner, Isabel. "Stephen Hawking Joins Boycott Against Israel." *New York Times*, May 8, 2013. Retrieved July 2013 (http://mobile.nytimes. com/2013/05/09/world/middleeast/stephen- hawking-joins-boycott-against-israel.html?from =homepage).

Larsen, Kristine. *Stephen Hawking: A Biography*. Amherst, NY: Prometheus Books, 2007.

McDaniel, Melissa. *Stephen Hawking: Revolutionary Physicist*. New York, NY: Chelsea House Publications, 1994.

McEvoy, J. P., and Oscar Zarate. *Introducing Stephen Hawking: A Graphic Guide*. London, England: Icon Books, 2005.

McGrath, Jane. "10 Cool Things You Didn't Know About Stephen Hawking." How Stuff Works. Retrieved June 6, 2013 (http://science.howstuffworks.com /dictionary/famous-scientists/physicists/10-cool -things-stephen-hawking.htm).

McPherson, Stephanie Sammartino. *Stephen Hawking*. Minneapolis, MN: Twenty-First Century Books, 2007.

Myint, B. "Modern Minds That Changed the World: Stephen Hawking." Biography.com, September 18, 2012. Retrieved August 20, 2013 (http:// www.biography.com/blog/modern-minds-that -changed-the-world-20972873).

PBS.com. "Stephen Hawking." 1998. Retrieved May 10, 2013 (http://www.pbs.org/wgbh/aso/databank/ entries/bphawk.html).

Redd, Nola Taylor. "Black Holes: Facts, Theory & Definiton." Space.com. Retrieved June 6, 2013 (http://www.space.com/15421-black-holes-facts -formation-discovery-sdcmp.html).

INDEX

ABOUT THE AUTHOR

Mary-Lane Kamberg is a professional writer, who specializes in nonfiction for young readers. She is the author of *Understanding the Elements of the Periodic Table: The Transition Elements*, as well as the biographies *Bono: Fighting World Hunger and Poverty* and *All About the Author: Margaret Peterson Haddix.*

PHOTO CREDITS

Cover, p. 1 Menahem Kahana/AFP/Getty Images; p. 4 NASA/JPL-Caltech/UCLA; p. 5 Miguel Riopa/AFP/Getty Images; p. 7 Gary Houston/Wikipedia/File:20040409-003-abbey-gateway.jpg/ CC0 1.0; p. 9 DEA Picture Library/Getty Images; pp. 10–11 Universal Images Group/Getty Images; p. 14 Steve Jurvetson/Wikipedia/File:Milky Way Night Sky Black Rock Desert Nevada.jpg/CC BY-SA 2.0; pp. 20–21, 34–35 iStock/Thinkstock; pp. 22–23 Bloomberg/Getty Images; p 25 Getty Images; p. 27 Courtesy ICTP Photo Archives; p. 30 David Levenson/Getty Images; p. 37 The India Today Group/Getty Images; p. 39 Bob Mahoney/Time & Life Pictures/Getty Images; pp. 44–45, 78–79 NASA/JPLCaltech; pp 48–49 Richard Kall/Science Source; pp. 50–51 Homer Sykes Archive/Alamy; pp. 52–53 David Montgomery/Hulton Archive/Getty Images; pp. 58–59 Sacramento Bee/© Randall Benton/ZUMA Press; p. 61 Rex Features via AP Images; p. 63 Steve Kagan/Time & Life Pictures/Getty Images; pp. 67, 70, 88 © AP Images; pp. 74–75 Zero Gravity Corp/AP Images; p. 81 Mike Flokis/Getty Images; pp. 86–87 Yoav Lemmer/AFP/Getty Images; p. 91 NASA, Paul E. Alers/AP Images; cover and interior design elements Featherlightfoot/Shutterstock.com (fractal patterns), © iStockphoto.com/Rastan (stars), RoyStudio.eu/Shutterstock.com (canvas texture).

Designer: Michael Moy; Editor: Jeanne Nagle; Photo Researcher: Nicole DiMella